CW00432507

MOVIN' UP

REAL ESTATE RESCUE COZY MYSTERIES,
BOOK 2

PATTI BENNING

SUMMER PRESCOTT BOOKS PUBLISHING

Copyright 2023 Summer Prescott Books

All Rights Reserved. No part of this publication nor any of the information herein may be quoted from, nor reproduced, in any form, including but not limited to: printing, scanning, photocopying, or any other printed, digital, or audio formats, without prior express written consent of the copyright holder.

**This book is a work of fiction. Any similarities to persons, living or dead, places of business, or situations past or present, is completely unintentional.

CHAPTER ONE

Flora Abner lay on her bed in the tiny office room on the first floor, her heart pounding in her chest. It was late, sometime past midnight, but she felt wide awake. Wide awake and terrified.

Her eyes were on the ghostly white form of her cat, a fluffy Persian cat named Amaretto. The cat was crouched in the window, staring outside with an intensity Flora knew meant she had seen something. The same something that had woken her up. She wasn't sure if it had been a noise, or a shadow moving across her window. All she knew, with terrible certainty, was that someone was out there.

The first night it had happened, she had brushed it off as a bad dream until she saw the footprints in the soft soil at the edge of her driveway the next day. They dragged through the soft soil, as if whoever had left them had been shuffling their feet. She wondered if it was an attempt to hide the details of their shoeprint. Whoever was creeping onto her property at night had been tormenting her for the past week straight, always coming at a different time, but somehow never failing to wake her up.

She had only lived in this house for a month, which meant she had been dealing with this for a quarter of her time there. It did not put her in a good mood.

When Amaretto shifted, her head moving to track movement outside, Flora slipped out of her bed and walked barefoot over to the window, trying to keep back far enough that if someone was looking at the house, they wouldn't be able to see her.

It took a moment to figure out what the cat saw, but finally, her eyes caught the motion of someone walking along the shadowed edge of the forest her property bordered. There was no doubt that the trespasser was a person, but they were too far away, and it was too dark out for her to make out any details besides the humanoid shape.

After watching for a moment, she returned to her bedside table and unplugged her phone. After turning the screen's brightness down as far as it would go, she went over to the window, raised it so the camera was pointing at the forest, and pressed the button to start recording a video.

The flashlight came on. Swearing, she quickly exited the app and stepped back from the window. The bright light had blinded her in the darkness, and by the time her eyes cleared, the shadowy form was gone.

Another night with no proof to show what was happening. She would call Officer Hendricks again in the morning so he could make a note in her file, but she already knew there wouldn't be anything else he could do. The man had come out twice already, and she suspected he was beginning to think she was just being paranoid and jumpy, a city girl having trouble adjusting to living in the country.

Unsettled, Flora returned to her bed. As had become her habit this last week, she had gone through the house before she retired for the evening, making sure the doors and windows were locked. On top of that, her bedroom door was locked. If someone did break in, she would have time to escape out the window before they got into the room.

The safety precautions only made her feel a little better, and she knew from experience it would take her a while to get back to sleep. And then, tomorrow night, she would have to do this all over again, leading to a horrible cycle of sleepless exhaustion.

She woke up later than she usually did, with the sunlight streaming through the window and Amaretto staring at her impatiently from the pillow beside her head. She hadn't been sleeping well all week and was getting used to the feeling of hazy disorientation when she woke.

What she wasn't used to was the sound of polite knocking at her front door.

"Shoot," she said, sitting upright in bed and grabbing her phone. It was almost ten in the morning, an unfortunate side effect of her sleepless night. She wasn't expecting anyone this morning, but there were only a few people it could be. Considering that Grady wasn't able to come over until later this afternoon and she hadn't called Officer Hendricks yet, she would put her money on it being Beth York, her closest neighbor.

Beth was not someone she wanted to see while still wearing her pajamas at ten o'clock in the morning.

She got dressed quickly, pulling clothing off her portable clothes rack, and slapping together an outfit of jean shorts and a T-shirt, and pulling her hair back into a messy bun in an attempt to disguise the fact she hadn't brushed it yet. She hurried out of the bedroom as the knock sounded again and spotted her neighbor's face through the pretty glass panel of her brand-new front door. She forced a smile to her face, hoping it wasn't obvious she had just woken up.

"Hi, Beth," she said as she opened the door. "Is everything all right?"

"Oh, I was just out walking with Sammy," the woman said, bending down to pat the droopy-eared basset hound Flora rarely saw her without. The dog looked up at her and gave a single, slow tail wag before flopping down onto his side on her porch. "I noticed you haven't made much progress with your lawn. Are you sure you don't want me to give you the number of the young man who takes care of our grass?"

"No, no," Flora said. "I'm going to start working on it soon. Today, in fact. I finally found a mower to buy, and Grady is supposed to bring it over this afternoon."

"That's wonderful news," Beth said. She was an older woman, with tightly curled gray hair and keen eyes that didn't seem to miss a thing. She and her husband, Tim, had brought Flora a pie a week after she moved in, and after that, the woman had found an excuse to drop in almost every day. Flora wouldn't have minded, except every visit seemed to be a poorly disguised chance for Beth to criticize her house and property. "Do you want me to send Tim over to help you pick up the sticks in your yard? I don't think he has any other plans for today. He would be happy to help."

That was another thing about Beth and Tim. They were both retired, which meant they could and did stop by at any point during the day.

"No, no, don't bother him," Flora said. "I was just about to start doing it myself. In fact, I'd better get to it. It was nice to see you, though. I hope you and Sammy have a nice walk."

"Well, if you change your mind, just let me know. You take care of yourself, Flora." She eyed Flora's messy hair and the bags Flora was certain she had under her eyes. They stared at each other for a moment before Beth smiled and walked away, tugging on Sammy's leash. The dog heaved himself to his feet and followed her at an amble.

Flora retreated inside her house and shut the door with a sigh. She supposed her plans for the day were settled. What she *wanted* to do was work on taking down the wallpaper in the entrance hallway, but she knew if she didn't get started on the yard today, Beth would make good on her threat to send Tim over. The older man was perfectly nice, but he had a horrible habit of mumbling everything he said and kept up a steady stream of conversation that he expected regular responses to—all while having very strong opinions on everything Flora said or did.

No, she would much rather work on the yard on her own. At least it was a nice day, and Grady would be here later with her mower, and she had a pitcher of ice-cold lemonade waiting for her in the fridge.

She just wished she didn't feel so tired. On top of that, she knew she was going to be looking over her shoulder every second she was outside, on the off chance her nighttime visitor decided to make an appearance during the day.

CHAPTER TWO

Summer in Kentucky was hot. Sure, it got hot in Chicago too, but when she lived in the city, Flora never had to be outside for too long. She spent most of the day at an air-conditioned office, or in her equally air-conditioned apartment building. The most she had to deal with the summer heat was a brief walk down the sidewalk to the little coffee shop on the corner, or a morning's jog in the park.

The heat was different when she couldn't escape it. The ancient window air conditioner in the living room was the only source of cooling in the house, and it only got the temperature down a bearable amount when she had all the curtains drawn and the house was dark. It was also loud enough that when she was outside, she could hear it running from the road. The lack of central air was one reason she had kept her bedroom on the first floor instead of claiming one of the larger bedrooms upstairs. Heat rose, and the upper floors of her house were sweltering, even at night.

After the first half hour of scouring her yard for stones and sticks that might hurt her new lawnmower, she retreated inside, poured herself a glass of lemonade, and sat in front of the living room air conditioner, wondering if it was worth it to get a new one. It was just so hot, and not being able to escape from the heat was driving her insane. She didn't know how anyone could expect her to get yard work done in weather like this. She would have been tempted to put it off for an overcast day despite what Beth had to say about it, but the humidity on cloudy days was almost as bad as the sunshine on clear ones. No matter what she did, it seemed she was going to be sweating through it.

It was tempting to just call someone and have them do the work for her. But that wasn't the point of this. She had limited funds, but more than that, she wanted to learn to work with her own hands. If she gave up at picking up some sticks, how would she ever do anything more difficult?

With that thought bolstering her, she went back outside and continued dragging fallen tree limbs and smaller sticks off the grass. The property extended into the woods as well, but she had barely explored back there. There was a small pond hidden in the trees, which would have been nice to swim in, but it was green and murky. Getting it cleaned up and making nice paths through the forest would be a lot more work than just clearing the yard of debris, so it was unfortunately far down on her to-do list.

She wasn't sure what to do with all of the sticks and branches she found, so she decided to drag them just past the tree line and figure out a more permanent solution later. Maybe, once she had tamed the yard a little bit, she could have a bonfire and invite Grady, Violet, and some of Violet's friends.

It was afternoon by the time she reached the back third of the yard—she knew she probably would have been done already if she hadn't taken so many breaks, but the cool, dark living room was too tempting to resist for long. She was dragging a particularly heavy branch when she heard the sound of a car approaching along the road. She paused and shaded her eyes as she looked over toward the house, where Grady's truck was pulling into her driveway. She waved at him, then resumed hauling the branch, figuring she could go say hi to him when she was done. He had become something of a work friend to her over the past month. He had helped her with a handful of smaller projects, and they chatted together while they worked, and sometimes he stayed for something cold to drink after, but they hadn't hung out outside of that yet.

Violet was her best friend in town. The woman was only a few years younger than her and owned what was easily the best coffee shop in the area, Violet Delights. The interior of the shop was decorated in different shades of purple, and Violet herself often wore purple contacts, insisting that she wanted to fit in with the theme of the coffee shop, which she had named after herself. She'd gone out to lunch with Violet and her friends a few times but didn't feel like she had really clicked with anyone else yet. It was obvious she was an outsider—most of the other people in Violet's group of friends had grown up here, in the small town of Warbler, Kentucky. Flora was a little sad to think she would always be the odd one out, but she had to remind herself she would be leaving in two years anyway. She wasn't here to become a part of the town. She was here to fix this house up, flip it, and start over somewhere else.

She dragged the heavy tree limb into the woods, stumbling when her foot caught on a stone. Pausing to shake out her twisted ankle, she looked down and saw a strange, white rock half buried under the leaves. Something about the smoothness of it struck her as odd, and she dropped the branch, crouching to get a closer look at it.

She reached out, brushing dirt from the surface of the rock. It was a pale yellowish white color, and about the size of her ... head.

She froze as her eyes recognized the shape of what she was seeing. The smooth, rounded dome. The empty eye socket.

She jumped to her feet, screaming. Grady must have already been on his way across the yard because she heard running footsteps, and a moment later he burst into the trees.

"What happened? Are you hurt?" he asked, looking her up and down like he expected to see a horrible injury.

She met his blue eyes, knowing her own were terrified. Slowly, she extended a finger and pointed down at the ground, to the very human skull that she had partially unearthed.

She saw the moment he spotted it. His eyes widened, and he dragged his gaze from the skull back up to her.

"I'm not usually the superstitious type, but I'm starting to think you might be cursed," he muttered.

Carefully, he took her elbow and guided her in a wide berth around the skull. Flora couldn't stop staring at it.

Her mind flashed back to her nighttime visitor. She wasn't the superstitious type either, but after finding this skeleton, she had to wonder … had she seen a ghost?

CHAPTER THREE

Flora called the local police station's number instead of 911, since she wasn't sure if this qualified as an *emergency* emergency. The dead person was long, long past saving, after all.

She could tell the woman who answered the call was skeptical when Flora told her she found a human skull on her property, but she promised to send someone right out. Part of Flora wanted to go back and look at the skull again, to make sure she hadn't somehow mistaken it for something else. But as much as she tried to convince herself it was really a deer skull or even a bear skull, in her heart, she knew it wasn't. Grady confirmed it when she rambled to him about her doubts.

"Yeah, that was definitely human," he said.

They were waiting on her porch for the police to arrive. She had picked up a second camp chair a couple weeks ago, so she had a seat on the porch to offer to her guests, but she still wanted to get a swing or a nice bench seat for the porch. She knew she must be in shock, because it felt a lot safer to think about whether she should go shopping for one this weekend than it did to think about what she had stumbled across.

"I don't understand what it's doing on my property," she said. "Do you think this was a graveyard before someone built a house on it?"

"We've already got a graveyard. You pass it every time you go into town. I don't think there was ever a second one just a couple miles away—despite how it seems, we don't have *that* many people dying around here."

"Well, I'd rather live on an old graveyard than have someone stashing *dead bodies* on my property."

"It could be a lost hiker," he mused. "You're pretty close to state land."

"Or maybe it's just a Halloween decoration," she said hopefully. She would feel silly for calling the police if that was all it was, but her relief would be far stronger than any embarrassment.

"Maybe," Grady said, but he sounded doubtful.

When the patrol vehicle pulled up, its lights were flashing but the sirens were off, which was good because it meant Beth and Tim wouldn't be alerted to the incident. She knew they would find out eventually, but she would rather at least know whether she had actually found a real skeleton or not before they started asking questions.

She spotted Officer Hendricks through the windshield. He pulled the vehicle up alongside Grady's truck and shut the flashing lights off.

"Mr. Barnes," Officer Hendricks said, giving Grady the barest nod. Flora winced a little, hoping this didn't go as badly as the last time she and Grady had called the police together. Officer Hendricks had history with Grady's family, who were locals. She knew his brother was a troublemaker who was currently in prison, but not much beyond that. As far she knew, Grady himself hadn't ever been involved in anything illegal, and that was good enough for her.

"Officer," Grady muttered.

"Where's the skull you found, Ms. Abner?" Officer Hendricks said. He looked tired, and she suspected he thought this call would end up being nothing. This wasn't the first time he'd come out this week, but this time, she had something a little more serious than a footprint to show him.

"It's back here," she said, moving down the porch steps and around the side of the house. "Follow me."

As soon as she pointed out the area where she had found the skull, Officer Hendricks instructed her and Grady to stand back while he examined it. Pulling blue gloves onto his hands, he crouched down. She could tell by the expression on his face that it wasn't a forgotten Halloween decoration. It was a real skull.

His frown deepened, and he reached into the leaves to lift something the size of a wallet out of the dirt. As he rose to his feet and walked back over to them, she realized it *was* a wallet. He opened it and murmured the name he read inside. "Nick Smith. I can't believe *this* is where he ended up."

"You know who he is?" she asked.

"I know who this wallet belonged to, but we'll have to match dental records to be sure," he said, carefully zipping the wallet into a plastic bag. "This changes things. I need to get the forensics team out here. We'll be taping the area off, and I'm going to need both of you to either return to the house or leave the property. I'm also going to be going back over those reports I took down about your other problem, Ms. Abner, just in case it's related."

For a wild moment, she thought he was echoing her earlier thought about a ghost, but then she realized there was a much more *real* concern. "You mean, whoever keeps coming here might have been looking for the body?"

In her peripheral vision, she saw Grady's eyes narrow. She felt a pang of guilt. She hadn't wanted to worry him, so she had only mentioned the incident the second time it happened, and then had done her best to downplay it. He had offered to camp out in his truck in the driveway overnight and chase the trespasser if they came back, but she had wanted to handle it the official way.

All of a sudden, the issue seemed much more serious. If Officer Hendricks was right, this wasn't just someone looking to steal some tools or take a midnight stroll in the woods. It was someone who already had blood on their hands, someone who had a secret they wanted to hide.

"It's possible," Officer Hendricks said. "I strongly suggest you get some security, Ms. Abner. Motion sensor lights, an alarm, or even a big dog would be a good deterrent."

She had a feeling Amaretto wouldn't approve of a dog, but the other security measures sounded like a good idea. "I'll look into it," she said. "Do you really think there's a connection?"

"Seems like a mighty big coincidence if there isn't," he said as they started walking back toward the drive-way. "And I don't like coincidences." They walked in silence back to the cars, where Officer Hendricks said, "I've got to make a call in my cruiser. You two sit tight. I'll need a formal statement before you're clear to go."

She and Grady returned to the porch, and she sat in one of the camp chairs, clasping her hands together. She couldn't get rid of the feeling that her skin was crawling, as if someone was watching her.

Had someone really been walking around her property at night, looking for a buried body? The thought was terrifying. What would they do when they learned the body had been found?

"Are you all right?" Grady asked.

"I'm kind of worried I'm going to get my throat slit in my sleep, but I guess I'm hanging in there," she said.

"My offer still stands. I'll keep watch in the truck if you want."

She hesitated, then shook her head. "Actually, I think I'm going to find somewhere else to stay for the night. Tomorrow, I'll get a security system set up, like Officer Hendricks suggested."

"All right," he said. "Let me know if you need help installing it."

She gave him a brief smile. "I'll probably take you up on that. Thanks. I wish you would let me pay you."

He waved her off as he always did. "Nah. I'm happy to help out."

After contacting the police station, Officer Hendricks spoke with her and Grady separately. It only took a couple of minutes since there wasn't much to tell.

When she mentioned she was thinking of staying somewhere else for the evening, he told her to call the Ringwood Motel.

"We have people stay there sometimes if they need a safe place to go after witnessing a crime or if their home is a crime scene," he explained. "Just show the proprietor my card, and he'll give you a discount for the night."

She thanked him, glad for the recommendation. She didn't want to watch as the forensics team dug through her yard searching for bones, so she helped Grady unload the mower from his trailer, then put Amaretto into her carrier, packed a bag full of everything she would need for the night, and then headed out, tailing Grady back into town.

This wasn't how she had expected the day to go. As she drove, she wondered if Violet would be free after the coffee shop closed. She could use a friend.

CHAPTER FOUR

"You look like you could use some comfort food."

Violet came into the motel room, shutting the door behind her. Amaretto was sitting on the corner of the desk, her yellow eyes narrowed in displeasure at the invasion of the room she had already claimed as her personal space. Flora stroked the cat's back on her way by, and pulled out the desk chair, offering it to Violet with a gesture. Amaretto jumped down when Violet put the pizza box on the desk beside her, flicking the tip of her tail as she slunk away.

"Thanks for coming over," Flora said. "And thanks for bringing food. I'm starving." It was past when she usually ate dinner, and the pizza smelled amazing.

"No problem. I can't say it's every day a friend calls me to tell me they've been chased away from their house by a *skeleton* they found on their property. I'd think you were joking, but you look freaked out."

"I *feel* freaked out," Flora said, sitting down on the end of the bed. "I still can't believe I actually found a body in my backyard. It feels surreal."

"Do you know the identity, or is it a mystery?" Violet asked as she opened the pizza box. Artichoke and chicken—Flora's favorite. She was touched that the other woman had remembered.

"Some guy called Nick Smith. Officer Hendricks said he was the subject of a missing person's case a couple years ago."

Violet's eyes widened. "The police are sure it was him?"

"He said they will need to match his dental records to be completely sure, but the wallet he found had Nick's ID in it," Flora said. Violet held the pizza box out to her, and she grabbed a slice. "I suppose it could be someone else, but he seemed pretty certain about it."

"Yeah, I guess that makes sense. Wow. I can't believe he's been dead all this time."

"Did you know him?"

Violet made a seesawing motion with her hand. "Sort of. You remember Harriet? She's one of the ladies who met for the Saturday brunch last weekend. The one with the curly blonde hair."

"Yeah, I remember her. She's a librarian, right? She seems nice."

"She is. She and Nick were… Well, it's a little complicated. They went on a couple dates, but she didn't like him enough to keep seeing him. He didn't get the memo, and for a while there before he went missing, she suspected that he was stalking her. She only told me about it after the fact, when he came up as a missing person. He worked at that feed store, the one I told you about when you asked me where you could buy cat food."

The mention of the feed store was a good reminder that she would need to stop by soon. Amaretto was running low on the cans of food she liked. "What happened when he went missing? Did the police suspect foul play?"

"I think the general consensus was that he just ran off. His car got repossessed a day or two before he disappeared, and Harriet told me she thinks he was deep in debt. The police looked for him, but I don't think anyone even mentioned murder as a possibility. Harriet was just relieved she didn't have to deal with it anymore."

"None of that explains how he ended up on my property," Flora said.

"Well, that place was sitting empty for a few years, wasn't it?" Violet asked. She had only come over once—Flora hadn't gotten the house put together enough to want to entertain.

She nodded. "It was empty for three years before I bought it. I think the old owner had someone come around occasionally to make sure no one had broken in, but there was no one doing regular maintenance on it for at least that long."

"Well, if people knew it was sitting empty, it might have seemed like a good place to hide a body," her friend mused. "If I'm remembering right, you don't have any close neighbors, and the road you're on is pretty quiet. If someone *did* kill Nick, they might have dumped the body there with the assumption the house would just continue to fall into ruin and the property would go untouched for decades."

Flora fought back a shiver. It was true that she didn't have any close neighbors—Beth and Tim's house was the only other one in view, and they were nearly a quarter of a mile down the road from her. If someone drove in at night with their headlights off, she doubted even someone as prone to peeking out their window as Beth was would notice.

"You don't think this will come back to me somehow, do you?" she asked. "Officer Hendricks said the trespasser I've been having problems with might have been looking for the body. Maybe they wanted to move it now that someone is living in the house?"

"Eugh," Violet said. "I can't imagine digging a body up after two years. If that's what was happening, though, it might be a *good* thing you found the body. The trespasser won't have a reason to keep doing it. If anything, they should want to stay away now. They won't want to do anything to draw attention to themselves."

Violet's words eased some of the concern that had been making her chest feel tight. "That makes a lot of sense, actually. I'll try to remember that tomorrow night, when I start jumping at shadows. I'm still going to get some new security measures, though. Grady said they sell some motion sensing alarms and cameras at the hardware store, so I'll swing by tomorrow and get something. I'll feel better knowing Amaretto isn't my first and only line of defense."

"Is he still helping you out at the house?" Violet asked as she held a piece of chicken out to Amaretto, trying to tempt the cat closer.

"Yeah, he's been great," Flora said. "I feel bad, though, because he still won't let me pay him."

"He's probably just trying to work up the courage to ask you on a date," Violet said. "I told you, that guy's been into you since the second he laid eyes on you."

Flora rolled her eyes. This wasn't the first time they had talked about this. Violet had *opinions* about everything, and Grady was one of them. "It doesn't matter, because I'm not dating. I'm a woman on a mission. Nothing is going to distract me from getting the house fixed up. Nothing except for skeletons, apparently." She wondered if she would ever feel completely comfortable on the property again. She was afraid some part of her was going to see human bones in every stray rock and stick.

"Don't you have to disclose that sort of thing when you're selling a house?" Violet asked. "My friend Eliza is a real estate agent, and she's mentioned that she has to disclose whether someone died on the property."

Flora frowned. She hadn't thought about that. "I'll have to look into it. I hope it doesn't bring the value of the house down too much." She groaned. "That makes me sound terrible, I know. A man is *dead*—I shouldn't be thinking of money right now. But … I've got a lot riding on this."

Her aunt had loaned her the money she needed for this new lease on her life, but she expected to be paid back. Flora needed to get out everything she put into the house, and more.

"Maybe if you spin it right, it can be a good thing," Violet suggested. "Use it to up the price and sell it to someone who's into morbid stuff."

She considered it for a second, then shook her head. "No, that wouldn't feel right. I don't want to profit off of someone's death. He's not just a skeleton—he was a real guy, you know? A person, with a life and dreams."

"A guy who was stalking one of my friends," Violet pointed out.

"But he still had a family," Flora said. "It wouldn't be right to do that to them. I'm sure his parents loved him, regardless of what sort of person he really was."

Violet considered that for a second, then nodded. "Yeah, you've got a point. It's not his family's fault he was a terrible person, and it's not fair to them to try to profit from something like this. I guess people tend to view their loved ones through rose-tinted glasses." She frowned. "Though I can't say I feel the same about my uncle. If I could denounce my relation to him, I would. You really haven't had an easy time of it since you came here, have you?"

Flora patted the bed and Amaretto jumped up beside her, rubbing her cheek against her owner's knee as Flora thought about the question. Just a couple weeks ago, Violet's uncle had attempted to murder her in order to keep another crime quiet. Flora had been expecting Violet to blame her for what happened, but instead, the other woman had been supportive of Flora and horrified by the lengths her uncle was willing to go.

"It's been good and bad," she said at last. "Today's leaning more towards bad, but overall… I'm still glad I moved here. Things will settle down eventually, I'm sure." She chuckled, feeling a little better already after the chat with her friend and a belly full of pizza. "Life has got to start looking up soon. It's going to be hard for whatever bad luck is following me to top a *skeleton*, of all things. No, I've got a feeling my lucky streak is about to start."

She hesitated, then reached out and knocked on top of the wooden desk just in case, ignoring Violet's laughter at her expense. She *wasn't* a superstitious person, but the recent events had shaken her, and she didn't want to tempt fate.

CHAPTER FIVE

The next morning, Flora checked out of the motel and drove directly to the police station. She had arranged a meeting with Officer Hendricks and was sent right back to his office when she got there. He raised an eyebrow when he saw Amaretto's cat carrier by her side but didn't comment on it.

"I had one of our new recruits parked outside of your house all night, but no one came by," he told her. "Forensics searched the entire area. We still have the location where the body was recovered taped off, and you're going to need to stay away from the area, but it should be safe for you to go back to the house itself. Have you thought about implementing any security measures?"

"Yeah, I'm going to stop at the hardware store later and buy a motion activated light and a security camera," she said. "At least that way, I'll be able to see if someone is out there."

"Good. If you *do* see someone again, call it in right away. Whoever has been trespassing is now a person of interest in a homicide investigation. I don't want to scare you, but you need to be aware of the danger. We don't know who this person is or what sort of mental state they're in, and we don't know if the discovery of the body will make them more unstable."

That was the last thing Flora wanted to hear, but she was glad he wasn't sugarcoating anything. For a second, she considered staying in the motel for another night or two, but she dismissed the idea. If she did that, when would it end? This was a two-year old case. It wasn't likely the police would be able to make quick progress on it, and she couldn't just avoid the house indefinitely.

"I'll be careful," she promised instead. "Are you sure the dead person is that Nick guy?"

"Sure enough that we've notified his next of kin," he said grimly. "This is not how I wanted his case to get resolved. You're free to go home, but I'm serious about you being careful."

"I will be. All I have to do is stay away from the crime scene tape, right?"

"That's correct. We had cadaver dogs go over your property, and they didn't find anything else, but if you *do* stumble onto something else you think might be connected to the case, don't hesitate to call." He handed her his card. "I know I already gave you one, but here, just in case you lost it. One of our patrol cars will drive past your house a few times a night for the next week, at least. Remember, we're here to help. I know the police have a bad reputation sometimes, but I hope you trust me when I say I really hate to see innocent people get hurt. Listen to your gut and don't hesitate to call if something feels off. I'd much prefer to waste half an hour on a false alarm, than have *your* murder be the next one I end up investigating."

"Jeeze, you're really boosting my confidence," she said dryly as she tucked his card away.

"Misplaced confidence gets people killed."

With that grim warning in her ears, she set off for home. She had shopping to do, but it was far too hot to leave Amaretto in the car, and the cat seemed eager to get home. She had to admit, it felt good to get back. The house might not really feel like home yet, but it was getting there, and it was comforting to see that everything was as she had left it. Well, everything besides the bright yellow crime scene tape in her back yard.

She took her things inside and let Amaretto out of the cat carrier. After setting up the cat's food and water, she pulled the living room curtains shut, turned on the air conditioner so it could start its endless battle against the day's heat, and then entered the kitchen to see what she had to make for breakfast.

No sooner had she opened the fridge than she heard a knock on the door. When she looked down the hall toward the front door, she wasn't surprised at all to see Beth peering in at her through the glass pane. Biting back a sigh, Flora went to unlock the door.

"Hey, Beth," she said. "Hi, Sammy."

The basset hound gave his customary tail wag, then lay down with a sigh.

"Good morning, dear," Beth said. "I hope I didn't interrupt anything. I just saw that your truck was back, and I wanted to make sure everything was all right. You had quite the police presence here last night. Tim and I were worried about you."

"Everything's fine," Flora said. She hesitated. Telling Violet about the skeleton was one thing, but Beth wasn't a friend, not really. However, Officer Hendricks had said they had notified Nick's next of kin. She had no doubt the story would come out soon anyway, so maybe it would be better to bite the bullet and get ahead of the story. "Well, I'm fine, but I discovered a body on my property. A skeleton, a human one, buried in the woods."

Beth gasped and covered her mouth with a hand. "Oh, how horrible." The keen interest in her eyes didn't seem to match her words. "You must have been terrified, you poor thing. Do the police know who it was?"

"They believe it was Nick Smith," she said. "He went missing—"

"Oh, I remember him," Beth said, cutting her off. "It was two years ago that he went missing, wasn't it? That poor young man, I always knew he wasn't going to end up anywhere good. I'm not surprised it ended the way it did for him. He asked my dear Tim for a loan once, while Tim was buying dog food at the feed store. It was terribly unprofessional. Tim declined, of course, but it made me wonder just how serious his money problems were."

"You knew him?"

The older woman nodded. "Of course. I used to teach as a substitute at the school, you know. I taught him when he was a young boy, fifteen or sixteen. He was a troublemaker back then. He and his friend used to sneak onto your property—this was long before you owned it, of course—and go swimming in the pond at night. It drove old Mr. Barton crazy, chasing them off."

Mr. Barton, she remembered, was the name of the old man who had owned her house before he passed away. His son was the one who had sold it to her. "Wait, he came onto my property? Like, a lot?"

"When he was in high school," Beth said. "You know, teenagers. That was over a decade ago, now. He cleaned up his act a little as he grew older. I do wonder how he ended up buried there. You'll tell me if you hear anything, won't you?"

"Of course," Flora said, only vaguely aware of what she was promising. Most of her thoughts were on Nick and his history with her property. Did it have something to do with his death, or was it a coincidence?

"Would you like to come over for some tea, dear? You look a little peaky."

Flora did not want to do that. She also didn't want to be rude, but luckily, she had an excuse. "I'm sorry, but I was just about to head back into town. I need to pick up a security camera and some cat food, and I really can't put it off, or my cat will never let me hear the end of it."

"I completely understand. My dear Sammy throws a fit if he doesn't get his dinner on time. Don't you worry; I'll keep an eye on your house while you're gone. If I see anyone who shouldn't be here, I'll let you know. The last thing you want is a bunch of lookie-loos trying to get a peek at where you found the body."

She thanked Beth, bent down to pet Sammy, and then leaned against the doorway and watched as Beth began the walk back to her house. The older woman seemed to mean well; Flora just wished she wouldn't drop by without warning at every hour of the day. Maybe, given enough time, she would get used to it.

She was getting ready to go out to town when her phone buzzed with a message from Violet.

Want to meet for brunch? Harriet and I are going to the diner. The two of you might benefit from chatting about Nick.

Flora hesitated, but she *was* curious about the dead man who had been buried on her property. Everything about Nick was a mystery to her. She might not be able to get answers about his death, or why his final resting place was on her land, but she could at least learn what kind of person he had been.

She sent Violet a quick text, promising to meet them, then headed out. She had a lot to do and hoped her earlier words to Violet were true. She didn't know how much more bad luck she could take.

CHAPTER SIX

Warbler was a small town, and in just the month since she moved here, Flora had memorized where almost everything was. She didn't need to use her GPS to find the feed store, she just followed the main road into town, turned left, made a right after a few blocks, and there it was. It was the closest thing to a dedicated pet store the town had, and she really hoped they had the brand of food Amaretto liked. The grocery store brand just wasn't cutting it.

She walked inside, feeling out of her depth. It was every inch a real country store, with a focus on supplies for livestock animals and things she might need if she was running a farm. She wandered around until she found the pet section, and then browsed through the cat supplies. They had a surprisingly good selection, and she was relieved to see the brand of food her cat preferred.

She grabbed enough cans to last for a week and grabbed a few cute cat toys to top it off. Amaretto had been upset by the move, and though she seemed to have settled in, she deserved to be spoiled.

She made her way to the register and had to clear her throat to get the cashier's attention. He had been staring at his phone as if the rest of the world didn't exist, and he jumped a little when he noticed her.

"Sorry," he said. "It's been a weird morning. Did you need help finding anything, or is this it?"

"This is it," she said, stacking the cans of cat food on the counter. "And no worries. It's been a weird day for me too."

He began scanning her items, glancing at her between each beep of the computer. After a few repetitions of this, he paused and said, "You're that woman, aren't you? The one who bought that old house on Robin Road?"

Flora's eyebrows rose. "That's me. How did you know?"

He resumed scanning the items. "Oh, you know. I just heard about you around town. I also heard there was some sort of issue with the police there last night. I hope no one got hurt."

As far as Flora knew, the only people who knew about the police response on her property were Beth, Tim, Violet, and Grady. She wasn't sure what to think of the fact that the news had apparently spread so quickly. *Small towns,* she reminded herself. *Things are different here.*

She opened her mouth to say, *No, no one got hurt*, but paused when she realized that wasn't true. Someone *had* been hurt, even if it had happened a long time ago.

"I found a body," she said instead. "Someone who was a part of a missing person's case a few years ago."

He paused again but finished ringing up her items without saying anything. She handed over her card to pay and thought he had dropped the subject. She was surprised when he said, "So, it's true then. They found Nick," as he handed her card back.

"Did you know him?" she asked.

He focused on bagging her items while he responded, not quite looking at her. "Yeah. He used to work here, you know? It was a big deal when he went missing. Do you know if the police have any idea what happened to him? I always wondered when and how he would turn up."

"I don't know much," she said, truthfully. "I think they're treating it as a homicide investigation. If you know anything that might help them figure it out, I'm sure the police would appreciate it if you talked to them."

"Oh, I don't know anything." He handed her the bag. "We weren't close, and he never really talked about his personal life at work. It's just weird to know someone I used to work with is dead. That's all."

"Right." She looped the plastic bag over her wrist and glanced at his nametag. "Well, thanks, Sydney. Have a good day."

"You too."

She left the feed store, glancing back only once to see that the man was watching her as she left. Shaking her head, she returned to her truck, tossing the bag on the passenger seat. Small towns were weird.

Violet and Harriet were already seated in the diner when Flora arrived, though they hadn't ordered yet. She sat across from them at the booth, and Violet made the introductions.

"I know you two already met, but it was just in passing. Flora, this is Harriet Norman. You'll see her plenty if you go to the library—she works there almost every day. Harriet, Flora Abner. She's a house flipper, and she's working on that old house I told you about."

Flora shook the other woman's hand. "It's nice to meet you, again."

"You too," Harriet said, smiling. She was a tall woman, with curly blonde hair Flora was instantly envious of. "Thanks for meeting us here. I'm sure you'd rather not talk about it, but Violet told me you're the one who found Nick. I just … is it really him?"

Flora bit back a groan. She had known, of course, that was the reason for this brunch, but somehow between replying to Violet and arriving here, it had slipped her mind. It seemed like everyone she spoke to today wanted to talk about the skeleton.

"I don't know. Officer Hendricks found his wallet, and he said he contacted Nick's relatives, but I think they still have to do some … forensic stuff to be certain. Chances are it's him, though."

Harriet slumped, and for a moment, Flora felt bad. But then, Harriet said, "I'm sure I'm going to sound like a terrible person, but I feel relieved. I've been wondering when he would turn up almost every day for these past two years. Now that it finally happened, I feel like I can relax. Did Violet tell you our history?"

"A little bit of it," Flora said.

There was a pause while the waitress came up to take their orders, then Harriet leaned forward, her elbows on the table, and said, "I feel like I should tell you, since you're the one who found him. We dated for about a month, and we just didn't click, so I broke things off. But he didn't take no for an answer. I never had any proof, not enough to get a restraining order, but I swear he was stalking me. I would see his car parked outside of my apartment building at all hours, and I always seemed to run into him when I was out and about in town. It was honestly the most terrifying couple of months of my life. When he disappeared, I was worried at first that he had gone off the deep end and was going to show up one day completely bonkers and try to kidnap me or something. I don't think anyone thought he was dead. I feel bad for his family, but I'm just really, really glad that I won't have to worry about him showing up out of nowhere anymore. Gosh, that makes me sound like a monster, doesn't it?"

"I'm sure Flora understands," Violet said, patting her friend's hand. "She's had similar experiences."

Flora wrinkled her nose. "Well, I wouldn't say my nighttime visitor is quite as intense as Harriet's experience was." Focusing on the blonde woman, she said, "Every night for the past week, someone's been trespassing on my property. I've never gotten a clear look at them or seen any actual evidence other than a footprint, but I know they've been there. It's been terrifying, but the police think it was related to the body—Nick's body. I'm hoping now that the body was found and recovered, they'll stop."

"I'm so sorry you had to go through that," Harriet said. "I completely understand how terrifying it is. If it doesn't stop, don't be shy about letting people know. I didn't tell anyone while it was happening, and

I should have. Give me a call if you ever need someone to talk to about this."

"That means a lot to me," Flora said. "Thank you."

They exchanged phone numbers and spent the rest of brunch chatting about lighter things. As they got up to leave, Flora shot Violet a quick, grateful smile. Violet had been trying hard to help Flora integrate into the limited social life of the town, and Flora was pretty certain she had succeeded here. Flora thought she had just made another friend, and though she wished the circumstances were different, she was glad to feel just that little bit less lonely.

CHAPTER SEVEN

She went to the hardware store after brunch. The day had grown overcast, and she smiled a little, thinking about the first time she had met Grady, when he helped her put a tarp over the hole in her roof. It was still up there and had successfully kept the interior of her house dry over the past month. He'd even helped her find a reputable company that was going to come out to repair and reshingle the entire roof soon.

The house was still a long way from where it needed to be, but she was making progress. It felt strange to think she was actually going to be able to do this. To take an old, rundown house that she had bought practically for pennies, and turn it into something beautiful, that people would want to live in. The house was getting a second lease on life at the same time she was.

The elderly Mr. Brant, the owner of the hardware store, was behind the counter when she went in. She waved at him, and he nodded at her. She was tempted to ask him where Grady was, but he was hard of hearing and any conversation she attempted to have with him would just devolve into shouting. Instead, she grabbed a cart and started walking the aisles until she found the small selection of home security devices. She was still standing there looking at the options when Grady found her a few minutes later.

"Glad to see you're taking this seriously," he said, his arms crossed and an amused look on his face. He never seemed busy when she came in, but then, none of the little shops in Warbler ever seemed very busy. The hardware store was no exception. "I heard you come in. You've been trying to decide what to buy for the past five minutes, haven't you?"

"There are a lot of options," she said. "And I've always been bad at making decisions. I was thinking, maybe some floodlights? I want them to turn on automatically if someone is walking by the house, but I realized a motion activated light would probably sense raccoons and opossums too, right?"

"You don't want raccoons or opossums poking around your house anyway," he pointed out. "So it's not bad if the lights scare them off. How many were you thinking?"

"Two?" She bit her lip, considering. "One for by the front door and one for the back of the house? Or do you think I should get some for the sides of the house too?"

He shrugged. "It just depends on how much you want to spend. Are you getting cameras too?"

"Yeah. I want one watching the driveway, and then one looking out over the backyard. I was also thinking of getting some type of audible alarm, but I don't think my neighbors would appreciate that."

"How about an air horn?" he suggested. "We sell them. People take them camping to chase away bears. It would give a person a good fright too."

"Perfect," she said. "I don't want to spend too much, but I don't want to get something that's going to break in a week either. What brands do you recommend?"

He helped her pick out the lights—four of them, one for each side of the house—and two security cameras that were supposed to have good night vision mode.

As she followed him to the aisle with the air horns, she said, "You're the first person I talked to today who hasn't wanted to talk about Nick. It's nice."

"Have you talked to many people so far this morning?" he asked, looking amused again.

"I'll have you know that I have a very busy social life," she said. She started counting down on her fingers. "I talked to Officer Hendricks before going home this morning, then Beth came over and wanted to hear about last night, then I went to the feed store, and the guy there recognized me. Apparently, he knew Nick too—they were coworkers. And after that, I had brunch with Violet and Harriet, and of course Harriet wanted to talk about him too, since they had a history together." She blinked, a little surprised that she'd had such a busy morning. She still felt like she didn't know very many people in her new town, but she'd already had five discussions with people she considered friends, or at least friendly acquaintances this morning. Sydney didn't count, since she had only just met him.

"Harriet Norman?" Grady asked, his expression morphing into a frown. "What did she have to say?"

What Flora, Harriet, and Violet talked about felt private. She trusted Grady, but it wasn't her place to share that information with him. "Just girl talk," she said. "I think she needed to hear the story directly from the person who found the body, instead of hearing about it secondhand."

"She was a person of interest in his case, back when he went missing," Grady said, his tone serious.

Flora blinked. "She was? And wait—how do you know that?"

"It happened before my brother went to prison. He used to date her sister, and they still talked." He shrugged. "Small town, remember?"

"Right. Why was she a person of interest, though? I thought no one suspected foul play."

"I just know the police brought her in and questioned her a few times. They had a bad breakup right before he vanished, which is probably why she was a person of interest to them."

That wasn't how Harriet had told the story, but she figured it was probably a matter of facts being twisted as rumors passed from person to person. "Well, she didn't have anything to do with it," Flora said. "I think she's just relieved to have closure."

Grady frowned but dropped the issue. "You said the guy at the feed store was Nick's coworker. How did he know about the body?"

"I guess he heard about the police response to my house?" she said, shrugging. "I'm not really sure. He must be friends with someone I told about it. For all I know, Beth is his grandmother or something. Honestly, nothing about this town surprises me anymore."

"Which one was it? Keith? Sydney?"

"Sydney," she said. "Do you know him?"

"Not well," he said, but he didn't elaborate further than that.

"I'm hoping all of this dies down soon," she said, letting the subject change. "I don't want to be known as the lady who found a skeleton in her yard for the rest of my time here. People will forget about it, right?"

She could tell by the expression on his face he was skeptical, but he just grunted and handed her an air horn. "Sure. If you want help installing all of this, I can come over after work. Around eight?"

"Perfect," she said. "I'll make something for dinner." He started to protest, but she said, "No, no. I owe you. You've been a lot of help."

She left the hardware store a few minutes later feeling positive. She had dinner plans, and by tonight, her security cameras would be installed. Tomorrow, assuming it wasn't another rainy day, she could get to work on the yard. She would just have to trust that the police had been thorough in their search for other unpleasant surprises. She wasn't sure she could take it if she stumbled across a second skeleton in as many days.

CHAPTER EIGHT

The rain started shortly after she got home. It wasn't a storm, just a steady patter on the roof and windows. She had stopped at the grocery store on her way back, and now she dropped the groceries off in the kitchen along with her bag from the hardware store before going back outside to move the riding lawnmower into the shed so it didn't get wet. She still didn't quite trust the shed, which looked like it might fall down if someone looked at it funny, but Grady had said it was safe enough for now, and she trusted *him*. The floor was dirt, and the mower kicked up dust as she rolled it inside and turned it off. Something about the murky, cobweb-filled interior of the shed always left her feeling uncomfortable. She tried to brush it off, telling herself there was no one else out here, no one but her and, a quarter mile down the road, Beth and Tim York, her kindly if sometimes frustrating neighbors. She was alone on her property and had nothing to worry about other than the spiders.

After the recurring issues with the trespasser, that attempt at self-reassurance fell flat. She tucked the mower keys into her pocket and hurried out of the shed, glancing toward the tree line as she half jogged through the rain back to her house. She didn't see anyone out there, and the trespasser had only ever come during the night, but the knowledge that someone *could* be out there made her uncomfortable. She was really, really glad she had those security cameras. Between those and the promise from Officer Hendricks that someone would be driving by in a squad car, she should be safe.

It was still only early afternoon, so after she put away the groceries, she took out her laptop and rewatched an instructional video about removing wallpaper. The wallpaper in the entry hall might have been pretty once, but now the floral design was faded and yellowing, and it was peeling at the seams. It needed to go, so she changed into something she wouldn't mind getting dirty, put on some music, and got to work.

It wasn't an unpleasant job, exactly. It smelled nice, since the video she had watched instructed her to use a mixture of liquid fabric softener and warm water to soak the wallpaper before she removed it with a putty knife. It was still hard work, and her arms got tired more quickly than she liked.

She managed to get half the hall done before she had to call it a day and start on dinner. She took a quick shower and put on something nicer, then went into the kitchen to start the food. She was a very average cook, but she could follow a recipe, and was following a new one for spaghetti with giant meatballs. She would also make a fresh salad, and she had a tub of premade cookie dough so she could make chocolate chip cookies for dessert.

By the time she heard Grady's knock at the door, the meatballs were in the oven, and the house smelled pretty darn good. Amaretto had spent the last half hour watching her from one of the chairs at the kitchen table—the cat wasn't allowed on the table or the counters, but chairs were fair game, and she had claimed one of them for herself. Flora double-checked that she had set the timer, then washed her hands and went to answer the door. She hadn't realized how tense being alone here had made her until something in her relaxed at the sight of Grady's face through the glass panel in the door. She smiled as she let him in.

"Hey. How was the rest of your shift?" she asked as he took off his boots. She had bought a rack for shoes a couple of weeks ago, and he put them on the bottom shelf before coming all the way in and closing the door behind him. She had cracked open the living room window to let in the smell of rain, and the air conditioner was off and blessedly silent.

"The same as always," he said. He crouched down to hold out a hand to Amaretto, who sniffed his fingers delicately, twitched her tail, and then padded away. Flora chuckled as he rose to his feet.

"She'll come around."

"Seems like she thinks she rules the roost."

Flora smiled because Grady knew full well she spoiled her cat—she had treated him to a rant about how the local grocery store didn't stock Amaretto's favorite brand of food, and over the course of the rant, his expression had changed slowly from pure bafflement to outright amusement.

"Just look at her little face and her little whiskers and her tiny little toes. Doesn't she deserve to be spoiled?"

"Cat people," Grady muttered, shaking his head, but she saw the smile on his lips. "You're all crazy."

"You're just jealous that she won't honor you with her affection," Flora said, grinning. "Dinner will be ready in about forty-five minutes, I think. That should give us time to get everything installed, right?"

"Right," he said. "Do you have your tools?"

With his help, she had been slowly building quite the collection of basic tools, and now she took her toolbox out from where she kept it at the top of the basement stairs. She emptied the bag from the hardware store on the kitchen table, and the two of them spent a few minutes poring over the instructions before they went out onto the front porch to install the first floodlight and the security camera. The lights were solar powered, which meant they wouldn't work too well this first night since it was already evening and overcast to boot, but the security cameras needed to be plugged in, so she had to dig through some of the boxes she had yet to unpack to find an extension cord. The cameras connected to Wi-Fi and had an app she could download on her phone so she could see the security feed from anywhere. Grady moved the camera around while she looked at the footage through her phone until he found the perfect angle, which looked out at the driveway, the front yard, and the porch steps.

"Perfect," she said. "Don't move it an inch. I'll come drill the screws in."

They set up the other camera by the back door, where it looked out over the back yard and the shed. She hoped the two angles would be enough to catch any trespassers, but at least if someone tried to get into the house, the cameras wouldn't be able to miss them. They installed the other floodlights around the house before going inside so Flora could finish making dinner. While they ate, Flora kept flicking through the two video streams on her phone, wishing she had done this back when she first moved in.

"This is so cool," she said. "I can see everything. If the trespasser comes back, they're going to be in for a surprise. Oh, how do you like the food? I've never made meatballs before."

"It's good," he said. She believed him, since he had already finished most of his plate. "You're a good cook. Thank you."

"I'm really not, I'm just decent at following instructions. Whenever I try to make something without a recipe, it goes … well, badly is a nice word for it. I'm glad the meal turned out well, though. Like I said, I owe you. You've been a huge help. I can't tell you how much I appreciate it."

"You don't owe me anything," he muttered. "I'm glad to help. Are you going to feel safe here tonight?"

She nodded. "I already feel safer than I have all week. Between the security cameras, the floodlights, and Officer Hendrick's promise about a patrol car driving by during the night, I think I'll be okay."

"Still, call me if something happens. I don't mind, even if you wake me up."

"All right," she promised. "Thanks, Grady. If I need to, I will. But I really hope nothing happens. This is my house, you know? I want to feel safe here."

Grady left after the meal, and Flora tidied up a little before shutting the windows and locking the doors. She retreated to her bedroom, where she watched a few episodes of a TV show she liked on her laptop, Amaretto sprawled out beside her. When she wanted to, the cat could take up a lot of space, and Flora never had the heart to make her move.

When she started getting tired, she made sure her phone was plugged in and the air horn was in reach on her nightstand before turning on her side and closing her eyes. She wasn't sure what time it was when her eyes snapped back open and she saw Amaretto silhouetted in the windowsill, staring intently at something outside.

Dread crept into Flora's heart. She reached for her phone, and saw some missed notifications from the security camera app. Both of them had caught motion in the last few minutes.

Even though it made her feel like a child, she pulled the covers up over her head and huddled underneath them before tapping on the screen to open the app. She checked the live feed for both cameras but didn't see anything moving on them, so she went to the recordings and scrolled back to the first clip of motion that had set the camera on the porch off.

The video showed someone walking across her driveway. Flora swore she felt her heart freeze in her chest, but that shadowy form wasn't all there was. A *second* form followed the first one, moving at a slow, unsteady pace.

Hold on. She frowned and paused the footage, then zoomed in. She let it play frame by frame. Something about these two figures seemed familiar. It wasn't until they passed directly in front of her porch and the screen lit up a little—the solar-powered floodlight must have weakly come on at the motion—and they both looked over that she realized who they were.

Her nighttime trespassers were her next-door neighbors, Beth and Tim York.

CHAPTER NINE

The instant she recognized them, all of Flora's fear left in a rush, only to be replaced with anger. She didn't know what they were up to, but she had been living in fear for *weeks* because of these two. She had even told Beth about the trespasser, and the older woman had patted her on the arm and assured her it was probably nothing.

Livid, Flora swung her legs out of bed, grasping her phone tightly in one hand. She paused, eyeing the airhorn, but as angry as she was, she didn't want to accidentally give either of them a heart attack. She left it on her bedside table and yanked her bedroom door open, stepping out into the living room. Pausing only to shove a pair of shoes onto her feet, she stepped out through the front door and then realized she had no idea where they had gone. In the video, it looked like they were going around the side of the house, so she headed off in that direction.

The moon was half full and illuminated her yard well enough that she could see the two of them making their way over to where the crime scene tape was. Flora hurried after them, calling, "Hey! What are you doing?"

Beth and Tim both paused, then turned around to face her and started walking back across the yard to meet her.

"Oh, Flora, whatever are you doing up at this hour?" Beth asked, as if they had run into each other on the road at an early hour of the morning.

"I installed security cameras because I'd been having issues with trespassers," Flora said, crossing her arms. "And lo and behold, it turns out my mysterious tres-passers were the two of *you*. I told you about this, Beth. I told you how scared I was. Why are you doing this?"

She blinked, wishing the tears pricking her eyes would go away. She felt … betrayed. Sure, she didn't know Beth well and she had often wished the older woman wouldn't drop by at all hours of the day, but she thought they were something like friends.

"It's not what you think, dear," Beth said. She reached out to grab Tim's hand and hesitated. The older man gave her a confused look. "We were just… I wanted to see the spot where you found the body. My knitting club—"

"No," Flora said. "I don't care. First of all, it's a crime scene. Even *I'm* not supposed to go back there. Second of all, it's the middle of the night. And third … this is my property. You've no right to go walking around back here without my permission, and I certainly didn't give it to you. Just … just leave. Before I call the police."

"Surely it doesn't have to come to that," Beth said quietly. "Flora—"

"I don't want to hear it," Flora gritted out. "Just leave, please. If I see you again, I *will* call the police. I have security cameras now, and they record any motion automatically, so don't think I won't notice. Whatever's going on here, it ends tonight."

Beth hesitated, but she must have seen the resolution in Flora's gaze, because she relented, saying only, "All right, let's go home, Tim. I'm in the mood for some tea before bed."

They started walking back toward the road. Flora trailed along behind them, fuming, and hurt and wondering how she had been so wrong about Beth. She almost wished it had been someone else, though at least Beth and Tim weren't a danger to her. The last thing she wanted was to spend the next two years at odds with her closest neighbors. She just didn't understand *why* they had done this.

She followed them back to the road and stood at the edge of her property, watching until they were well on the way back to their own house. Then, she turned around and went back inside, locking the door firmly behind her.

She didn't think sleep was going to come easily tonight. Anger would keep her awake just as much as fear had.

She was still upset in the morning, though a bit of sleep and distance from the incident had improved her mood somewhat. She fed Amaretto breakfast, made herself some scrambled eggs and bacon, and picked at her food while she tried to make plans for the day. It was supposed to be clear today, so she would be able to start mowing the front half of the property. She would have to wait to do the back portion until the crime scene tape was taken down, but it would be nice to get the part near the road looking nice. It shouldn't take more than an hour or two, so she should have time to finish removing the wallpaper in the hallway too. It would be good to have that done and be able to start painting.

She picked up her phone, idly checking the notifications she had missed overnight. The sight of another recording from the security cameras made her blood run cold. Then she pressed play and saw that it was only a raccoon, scuttling out of the woods and into her shed. Where it stayed. Her eyes narrowed. There was no video of it leaving, which meant the critter was snoozing the day away inside her shed.

She was all for wild animals living in the woods where they belonged, but making a nest in her shed was another matter entirely. It seemed she had another problem to solve, though at least this issue wasn't as pressing as the leaking roof had been.

She knew just who to call for help. A glance at the clock told her the hardware store wouldn't open for almost another hour, so she dialed the number to Grady's landline.

"Hello?"

"Hey, it's Flora," she said. "I didn't wake you, did I?"

"No, I've been up for a bit. Did anything happen last night? Did the security cameras work?"

The question sidetracked her. "They did. I caught my neighbors, the Yorks, trespassing. I confronted them, and I don't think it will happen again."

He was silent for a second. "What did they want?"

"Just to take a peek at the crime scene, I guess. I know Beth likes to be involved in everything, but I have no idea why she thought the middle of the night was the time to do it. I was pretty upset when it happened. I still am."

"Did you tell the police?"

"No. Like I said, I don't think it'll happen again."

He hesitated. "Well, I think you should. It might be important."

"You mean, you think they could have something to do with the skeleton I found?" she asked. "Grady, I really cannot see Beth or her husband doing anything like that. I might be upset at them for trespassing, but they're harmless overall."

"I'm just saying," he muttered. "You don't really know them. You've only been here for a month. I don't know them well either, but I do know something seems off about all of this. You know I'm not a big fan of Officer Hendricks, but he'd want to know about this."

She sighed. "Fine, I'll stop in and tell him about it, but I'm not going to press charges. I just... I really don't think this has anything to do with the murder, and I don't want to cause more problems with them."

She wasn't happy about it, but she knew he was right. Officer Hendricks would want to know about this. She just hoped it didn't get back to her neighbors. As upset as she had been last night, she didn't want them as enemies.

"I also think I have a raccoon problem," she said, remembering the reason she had called him in the first place. "The back camera caught one sneaking into my shed last night, and it didn't catch it leaving. I don't want to play host to a raccoon family. What should I do?"

"You can shoot them if they're being pests."

"I don't want to kill it," she said. "It should be able to live out its life in peace. I just don't want it in my shed."

He sighed. "Get a live trap, then. You can trap it, and I'll let it go somewhere else."

"Perfect," she said. "Do you sell them at the hardware store?"

"No, you'll want to try the feed store. You'll need bait —a can of cat food should do. You can get the cheap stuff; I don't think a raccoon will be as picky as your cat. Though I'm sure by the time you're done with it, it will be."

"Ha, ha," she said dryly. "I guess I'll go into town and run some errands before I get started on the yard, then. Thanks, Grady."

Trying to ignore the lingering anger and hurt she felt about Beth, she finished her meal quickly. It was time to get to work.

CHAPTER TEN

She called Officer Hendricks while she washed the dishes and asked if he had time to meet with her this morning. She wanted to talk to him in person, so she could make sure there wasn't any confusion about her not wanting to press charges. He agreed to meet her in half an hour, so she hurried to finish her morning chores and then headed into town.

Never before had she been so familiar with the inside of a police station, but she was beginning to feel almost comfortable in the Warbler police station. She spent a couple of minutes chatting with the woman at the front desk before Officer Hendricks came out to take her back to his office.

"I'd say it's good to see you, but being a frequent visitor here isn't usually a good thing. Did you have problems again last night?"

"Yes and no," she said. "Before we begin, I just want to be clear that I'm not pressing any charges. The situation is dealt with, but a friend of mine thought I should tell you about it anyway."

His eyebrows rose. "Well, consider me curious. I do have to warn you, depending on what you're about to say, I may have to move forward with charges regardless of your wishes. It doesn't work the way you seem to think it does."

"So, if I tell you someone came onto my property uninvited, you would *have* to press trespassing charges?"

"In this particular case, no," he said. "I take it your nighttime visitor came back?"

She sighed. "Yeah. Grady and I installed some security cameras yesterday evening, and the cameras caught the trespassers last night. I have the video, if you want to see it. The people involved were my neighbors, Beth and Tim York."

His eyebrows climbed even higher. He waited while she pulled up the video of them walking past her porch. After watching it, he said, "You said the situation has been handled. I take that to mean you confronted them?"

"I went outside to find out what was going on and to ask them to leave. They said they wanted to take a peek at the crime scene. I just—I feel so betrayed. Beth *knew* how frightened I was, and she and Tim were the trespassers all along. I don't understand how she could do this to me."

"I've known the Yorks for years," Officer Hendricks said. "Beth might be a busybody, but she's a kind woman. This doesn't seem like her at all. Did she admit to trespassing the other times?"

Flora hesitated. "No, but how many different people could be out there, traipsing across my property every night? I live in the middle of nowhere."

He sighed, looking down at her phone to watch the video again. "Well, I'll make a note in my reports. If this continues to happen, please let me know. I can go out to talk to them without any charges being pressed officially. I understand why you don't want to pursue this, and I hope this marks the end of the problems you've been having, but keep your guard up. My gut tells me there's more going on."

Flora frowned. "Because of the body, right? You still think the issues I've been having with trespassers is connected to Nick."

"I'm not at liberty to discuss the case with you, but it *is* currently an open homicide investigation, which should tell you all you need to know. We are taking it very seriously, and so should you."

With that cryptic warning, he sent her on her way. Grumbling as she started her truck, she made her way to the feed store, trying to focus on what she had to get done today. She spotted the same employee from last time at the register, and once again, he seemed distracted. Sydney didn't even look around when she came in, so she went to the cat food aisle to pick out a can of cheap food to put in the trap. Finding the live traps proved more difficult, and finally she had to admit defeat and go to the counter to ask for help.

"Excuse me?" she said. Sydney jolted and blinked at her. He had been staring off into the distance, lost in thought, and he had bags under his eyes. "Do you sell live traps? I need one that's big enough for a raccoon."

"Yeah," he said. "They're in the back, follow me."

He led her to the back corner of the store, where a selection of traps ranging from rat sized to large dog sized were half hidden behind some seasonal items. She chose one of the medium ones and carried it back to the register, where Sydney rang up the trap and the can of cat food. He typed something on the computer, and the machine beeped and cancelled the order.

"Oops," he muttered. "Sorry. I pressed the wrong button. That's the third time I've done that today." He rescanned her items.

"Rough day?" she asked, taking out her wallet.

"You've got no idea. Do you want a bag for the cat food?"

"No, I'll just put it in my purse," she said. "Do you have any tips for setting up a trap to catch a raccoon? I caught one sneaking into my shed with a security camera, and I'm hoping to get it out before it causes any damage."

"You'll want to set it up right next to however he's getting in. He's probably been drawn to the house since it's occupied now. He can smell the food scraps and cat food in your garbage, so make sure your garbage bin is securely closed. If the raccoons get into it even once, they'll never stop coming around."

"Thanks," she said. She accepted her receipt, tucked her wallet back into her purse, and grabbed the trap and the can of food. "Let's see if I can convince the little guy my home isn't a good place for him and his family to be."

She loaded everything up into her truck and pulled away from the feed store's parking lot. It was still morning, and the grass was still damp with dew and yesterday's rain, so she decided to swing by the library. Violet had said Harriet worked there almost every day, and she knew making friends took effort. She figured she could stop by, say hi, and pick up some books to read while she was at it.

The Warbler library was a small brick building near the town hall, a block away from the town's central intersection. The second she stepped in the door, she was enveloped in the scent of old paper. It felt cozy, even though she didn't remember the last time she had been in a library. Harriet was tapping away on the computer behind the front desk when she came in, but she looked up as Flora approached and gave her a bright smile.

"Hey," she said, her voice hushed. "Is this your first time here?"

"Yeah," Flora said, leaning against the counter. "What do you need from me, if I want to get a library card?"

"Technically, either your driver's license, or if you haven't changed your address yet, any piece of mail." She leaned closer conspiratorially. "Just write down your name and address, though. Everyone knows you moved into that old house. You don't need to prove anything."

"Small towns are a little creepy," Flora said, writing her name and address out on the scrap of paper Harriet gave her. "You're not the first person who's mentioned they know where I live."

"Sorry," Harriet said as she entered the information into the computer. "I didn't mean it to come across that way. People just like to talk."

"It's fine," Flora said. "I guess there isn't much else to do around here."

"Seriously. This town is dead after eight, even on weekends. The movie theater doesn't even play anything after seven. It's a Friday night, but there is literally nothing to do except go to one of the two bars in town."

"If you want, you and Violet could come over to my place tonight," Flora offered. It was spur of the moment, but she had enjoyed having Grady over the evening before, and she missed having a decent social life. She needed to make an effort if she was serious about wanting friends. "It might not be the same as a movie theater, but we can hook my laptop up to the TV, and I've got a microwave for popcorn."

"Really?" Harriet said. "I'd love to see your house. I hope that doesn't sound creepy, but I've seen the outside before, and I always wondered what it was like on the inside."

"Fair warning, it needs a lot of work, but I'd love to show you around."

"Thanks," Harriet said. "I'd love to come over. I get out of here at seven, but I'll probably want to go home and change first."

"How does eight sound? I'll text Violet and make sure it works for her too."

"Perfect. I'm actually looking forward to a Friday evening for once."

Flora had a spring in her step when she left the library, her arms full of new books to read. Making friends took effort sometimes, but it was always worth it. She was glad she was starting to have a social life again. Plus, having people around would make it easier to forget about Officer Hendricks's warning. He was probably wrong. Her problems with trespassers were almost certain to be over now that she had spoken to Beth about it.

CHAPTER ELEVEN

Flora stopped at the grocery store to pick up some popcorn and other snacks and stopped by the gas station to buy and fill up a five-gallon gas can so she could use the mower, then made her way home. She set the live trap up next to the hole in the side of the shed that the raccoon had let itself in through, then backed the lawnmower out. It already had some gasoline in it, but she filled the tank the rest of the way, then put the half-full gas can just inside the shed door.

She had never used a riding lawnmower before, but she had watched a video on how to operate this model and after a few minutes of uncertainty, she got the hang of it. Starting at the front of the property, she began the long process of cutting the lawn. The grass was high, and sometimes she had to backtrack to get a clump that she missed. It was slow going, but by the time she reached the midpoint of her yard and stopped so as not to go near the crime scene, she was amazed at the difference it made. She was beaming as she put the mower away. Sure, she was hot, sweaty, and covered in bits of grass and dust, but the feeling of achievement made none of that matter.

The grass looked amazing, but as a side effect, the flowerbeds and driveway looked worse than ever. The flowerbeds were filled with weeds, and the driveway was overgrown and almost more pothole than gravel. Still, the overall effect was a positive one. She glanced over at the Yorks's house, but she didn't see either of them outside. Trying to ignore the pang of betrayal in her chest, she went inside to shower, then started taking down the rest of the wallpaper in the hallway, humming along to music as she worked.

The work was hard, but she couldn't get over how *happy* she was. Getting this house fixed up wasn't easy, or even fun, but it felt deeply satisfying to her. She no longer woke up every morning with a feeling of dread at the thought of the rest of her life stretching out in front of her. She really hoped she could flip the house and make a career out of this. She was still learning, but her gut told her she had chosen the right path this time around.

She got the wallpaper in the hall done with time to spare. After bundling the scraps into garbage bags and putting them by the road, she swept the floors, tidied the living room, and then went upstairs to change into something a little more fun. She had the snacks and drinks laid out by the time Violet and Harriet pulled into the driveway – it seemed they had carpooled in Violet's car which, true to the ongoing theme in her life, was a pale purple color. She opened the door at their knock, letting them in off the porch. Violet took off her shoes while Harriet just looked around, taking it in.

"I love it," she said. "I can see what you mean about it needing work, but this house has beautiful bones. I love old houses. You're so lucky."

"It's going to take a lot of work to get it to where I want it to be, but it'll get there. Come on, I'll give you a tour."

She showed off her house, happily pointing out its flaws and telling the other women her plans for fixing it up. Violet had already been over once, and she complimented the small bits of work Flora had gotten done since the last time she was over. Having someone notice her hard work filled her with a warm sense of pride.

Soon, they settled down on the couch and Violet opened a bottle of wine. The conversation turned to the coffee shop, and then to Harriet's job at the library and an upcoming fundraiser. It felt good to just chat about the small things in life. Flora had missed this, and she was glad she was beginning to make some real friends in Warbler.

Violet gave her the login information for a video streaming service Flora wasn't subscribed to, and they put on a psychological thriller movie none of them had seen yet. A little after ten, when the movie was reaching its climax, the floodlight on the porch came on, making all three of them jump. Flora turned to look out the window behind the couch, but she didn't see anything moving outside.

"The sensitivity on the motion sensor must be too high," she said. "This is the first night they've had a chance to work, since we didn't install them until yesterday evening."

"Well, better too sensitive than the other way around," Violet said. "I'm glad you've got some security here now. I was getting worried about you."

"Why? I feel like I'm missing something," Harriet said.

Flora launched into the story about the issues with trespassing she had been having, reminding her what had happened. When she picked up her phone to show them the security footage from the night before, she paused, frowning. The security camera at the front door had recorded something a couple of minutes ago, back when the light turned on. She played the video and saw Tim shuffling past her front porch. Her fingers tightened on her phone. What was he doing here *again*?

"Sorry, I've got to go outside," she said. "I'll be right back in."

"What's happening?" Violet asked as she got up.

"It's my neighbor again. It's a long story, but I need to deal with this. You two stay in here."

"Hold on," Violet said. "I don't think you should go out there."

"I'll be fine," Flora said. "Here, you can keep an eye on the security cameras." She handed the phone over. "If anything does happen, call the police. But it's just my neighbors."

Before they could argue, she shoved her feet into her shoes, grabbed a flashlight, and stepped outdoors. The floodlight came on when it sensed her motion, and she jolted a little. She jumped a second time when she turned toward the driveway and saw Beth standing by her truck.

"Oh!" Beth said. She blinked in the sudden light from the floodlight and the flashlight. "Flora, thank goodness. I was just about to knock on your door."

"What are you doing here, Beth?" Flora snapped. "I told you, you can't keep coming onto my property without my permission. I *will* get the police involved if I have to."

"Hold on, Flora. You didn't give me the chance to explain before. It's not… It's not what you think. It's Tim. He has a condition where he gets more confused after nightfall. It's called sundowner syndrome. Sometimes he goes wandering or thinks he's somewhere other than where he is. Lately, he's been focused on your house. He seems to think he's living in the past—tonight, he muttered something about seeing Syd and Nick on old Mr. Barton's property again, and he hurried outside to chase them away before I could stop him. I swear, Flora, he doesn't know what he's doing, and he doesn't mean any harm by it."

Flora hesitated. "If that's what's been happening, why wouldn't you tell me this in the first place?"

"He's embarrassed about it, when he's thinking clearly," the older woman said. "He wouldn't want you to know."

Flora's shoulders drooped. "If that's what's been going on, of course I understand. Let's go get him. He must have gone around back, toward the—" She broke off, frowning. "Did you say Syd and Nick? Nick, as in the person whose body I found?"

"I did. I think I told you, he and his friend used to sneak onto this property at night and go swimming in that pond when they were teens. They lived just a couple miles down the road, neighbors. Old Mr. Barton went half mad chasing them off—he was afraid they were going to end up getting hurt or drowning, and it would be his fault. Tim was a younger man back then, and he would keep an eye out and come over to chase them off so Mr. Barton wouldn't work himself up over it."

"Syd as in … Sydney?" Flora asked.

Beth nodded. "Sydney Morrison. He grew up to be a fine young man, much better than that Nick, lord rest his soul. He's held a good job at the feed store for a long time now, and always asks after Sammy when we go in."

Flora blinked. Sydney had said he barely knew Nick, hadn't he? And he'd recognized her and knew where she lived, even though she hadn't ever met him before she stopped by the feed store to buy Amaretto's food. Goosebumps crawled up her arms, and she desperately wanted to try to figure out what all of this meant, but now wasn't the time for it. Tim was wandering around on her property in the dark, confused and lost in his own mind. Finding him was more urgent.

Behind Flora, the front door opened. She turned around in time to see Violet rush outside, her eyes wide as she rushed over to Flora and Beth, shoving Flora's cell phone into her face. Harriet followed behind her more slowly, though she looked equally as shocked.

"Something's going on," she hissed. "We were watching in the security camera like you said, when another notification popped up. From the camera in the back. There are people back there, Flora."

"I know, it's just Tim. Beth explained to me—"

"No," her friend said, cutting her off. "I saw two people, not just one. There's someone else out there."

CHAPTER TWELVE

Beth and Flora crowded around the phone to watch the brief recording, which showed one shuffling, shadowy form walking past the shed. Just as he reached the tree line, he paused and shook his fist at something unseen. The person he was confronting stepped out of the trees and seemed to talk to him. A moment later, both stepped into the shadows and vanished.

Beth gasped. "Tim!"

"Hold on," Flora said, reaching out to grab her sleeve before the older woman could rush away. "We'll go get him. But Violet and Harriet, I need you two to stay here and call the police, okay?"

"I'm not staying here if you're going out there," Violet said. "Are you crazy?"

"I'll stay," Harriet said, her hands shaking as she reached for the phone. "I'll call the police, and I'll keep an eye on the video footage from the cameras."

Flora hesitated, but having three people going after Tim instead of just two *would* be safer. "Okay. Tell them it's Sydney Morrison," she said. "He works at the feed shop. I think... I think he's the one who killed Nick."

Harriet's eyes widened. Flora clicked her flashlight on and she, Violet, and Beth hurried around the corner of the house. She swung her flashlight's beam across the backyard until the light caught two glowing eyes peeking out from her shed. Her breath caught in her throat, but in the next moment, the raccoon darted out of the shed and hurried toward the woods, bypassing the live trap completely. She could deal with that later. Entering the recently vacated shed, she grabbed two boards left over from the roof repairs she and Grady had done a month ago. She handed one to Violet and kept the other in her own hand.

"Just in case we need to defend ourselves," she whispered.

"Hurry," Beth said. "Tim could be in danger."

She swung the flashlight beam back and forth across the tree line as they walked across the property. The beam picked out the caution tape, yellow and flapping in the gentle breeze, but she didn't see any people. When Beth grabbed her wrist unexpectedly, she jolted to a stop.

"Look," the older woman said, pointing down.

There, in the leaves and the damp soil, were the strange, dragging footprints she had seen before. Footprints she now realized came from Tim, and his shuffling gait.

"They went past the tape," Flora whispered.

She hesitated only a moment before she ducked under the crime scene tape. Officer Hendricks wouldn't be pleased, but he would probably be less pleased if he had to investigate a second murder on her property, so she figured he would understand.

"Tim!" Beth shouted as they moved into the trees. "Tim, where are you?"

There was silence for a moment and then, "Beth? What are you—"

His voice cut off too suddenly. Flora swung the light in the direction his voice had come from just in time to see someone ducking behind a tree. She tightened her grip on the board in her other hand.

"Whoever's there, we see you. Come out. And don't hurt Tim."

Slowly, Sydney stepped out from behind a tree. Tim followed him, his eyes flitting over the three of them in confusion, the glare of the flashlight making him squint.

"Beth, love, did you hear the news? Nick died. That poor boy might have been a troublemaker, but he didn't deserve that."

"You're confused, dear," Beth said, hurrying over to take his arm. "Are you all right? Are you hurt?" She glared at Syd, who crossed his arms defensively.

"I didn't hurt him. What's going on?"

"I think that's a question *you* need to answer," Flora said. She wanted to cross her arms, but with the flashlight in one hand and the board in the other, it wasn't feasible. She settled for shining the light right at his face, and hoping he knew he was outnumbered by a lot of annoyed and armed women.

"I'm just—I'm looking for something," he said, shifting away from them.

"The police have been through here," Flora said. "They found everything there is to find, so they already have what you're looking for. You left something behind when you killed Nick, didn't you? Something that ties you to the crime."

"What?" He jerked back in surprise. "You think *I* killed Nick? He was my best friend."

"You said you barely knew him just two days ago."

"I shouldn't have," he said. "I felt bad about it as soon as I said the words, but I didn't *want* all the attention I knew would come when people remembered we were friends. It was bad enough dealing with it, without every customer asking me about it. You have to believe me. He was like a brother to me. I would never hurt him."

"Then what are you doing out here?" Flora snapped. "You're poking around at a crime scene in the middle of the night after kidnapping an old man, and you expect us to believe you're innocent?"

"I didn't kidnap anyone!" he said. "I was just telling Tim what was going on. I'm not the one who killed

Nick, but I think I know who did. Now that I know where his body was hidden, I'm going to find the proof I need to turn her in. I know it's a long shot, but I'm looking for an earring."

Beside Flora, Violet gasped. "Harriet?"

"What are you talking about?" Flora asked, shifting a little so she could see her friend.

"Harriet… She lost one of her favorite earrings. I remember her complaining about it, because it happened the same day we got the news that Nick was missing. She was frantic about it, and I didn't understand why—it wasn't an expensive one, just something she'd picked up at the mall. She was really shaken up. I didn't think much of it at the time, but looking back, she was shaken up *before* we heard about Nick."

Flora's eyes widened. "You think *she* did it?" She thought about it, trying to envision Harriet as a killer. "If he was stalking her, maybe it was in self-defense?"

"Stalking her," Sydney said, giving a disbelieving laugh. "You've got it wrong. Nick and Harriet dated for about a month before he called it off because she was too intense. But she didn't let him go easily. I'm the one who told the police they should question her. I thought either she drove him away, or she had something to do with his disappearance. They never found anything, though, and all this time, I never knew for sure."

Flora felt sick. She didn't know who to believe. The familiar brush of warm fur against her legs made her glance down, and she crouched automatically to run her hand along Amaretto's spine. As the cat mewed and arched her back, Flora froze.

"Amaretto? What are you doing out here?" Dropping the board, she scooped the cat up and held her close. "I don't understand. How did you get outside?"

"Flora," Violet said. "We—we left Harriet in the house. And if Sydney is right, she might guess what all of this is about."

Flora's eyes widened. She turned to Sydney. "You, come with us. Beth—just be careful, get Tim home safely."

She and Violet started running for the house, the cat still bundled up in her arms, and Sydney followed them. She wasn't sure what to expect, but it definitely wasn't the familiar, rich scent of gasoline. It became overpowering as they rounded the corner of the house nearest the porch.

Harriet was just setting the container of gasoline down when they came around the corner. They all froze, and Flora turned her head slowly to see the trail of gasoline leading inside her house, through the open door. She held onto Amaretto a little tighter, not sure whether Harriet had let her out on purpose or if it was just a lucky accident.

Slowly, Harriet reached into her pocket and pulled out a lighter. Her hand was shaking, but she managed to light it after two tries.

"What are you doing?" Flora said, her voice sharp with fear. "Are you going to burn my house down?"

"I need a distraction," Harriet whispered. "It's nothing personal, and for what it's worth, I wish this had never happened. I wish we could be friends. But a big fire like this will keep the police busy while I get away. As soon as you mentioned Syd's name, I knew someone would put the pieces together. You probably won't understand, but Nick and I were meant to be together. If I couldn't have him, no one could."

"You killed him," Flora whispered. "Why did you bury him *here?*"

"He used to take me to the pond on this property on romantic, late-night dates," Harriet said. "I asked him to meet me just one more time, for old times' sake. It was quick—I brought a gun with me, and he barely even registered what was happening. I held him while he died, so he wasn't alone." She touched her ear. "I must have lost my earring then, but it never surfaced. I was so scared, at first. I wasn't strong enough to move him, so I just buried him in the leaves, but no one ever found him, not until you moved in."

She didn't know what to say to that. Violet was staring at her friend in horror, and the only thing that seemed to be holding Sydney back was the threat of the lighter and the gasoline.

"If you come any closer, I *will* burn the house down," Harriet said. "Violet, throw me the keys. I was just going to leave, until I remembered we carpooled. I don't want to hurt anyone else. If you throw me the keys, I'll just go. I won't set the gasoline on fire. I promise."

Violet reached into her jeans pocket and took out the keychain. It dangled from her hand for a second. She met Flora's eyes, and Flora realized she had no idea what the other woman was going to do. Violet looked mad. Mad, and hurt.

"You were one of my best friends," Violet said softly. "First my uncle, and now you. I'm starting to wonder if everyone I know is a monster." She flung the keys away with all her might, and they landed in the road. "Get out of here, Harriet. I'd say something about how the next time I see you, you'll be behind bars, but that's a lie. I'm not going to visit you while you're in prison. I never want to see you again."

Harriet blinked back tears, but let the lighter go out and ran toward where the keys had fallen in the road. Before she reached them, a pair of headlights turned onto the dirt road from the main road, and Harriet froze.

The police car let out a chirp as it rolled to a stop in front of her, and a young policewoman rolled the window down, looking from Flora to Harriet and then back again.

"I had orders to patrol past this house tonight, but I've got to admit, I wasn't actually expecting to find anything unusual. Could one of you lovely ladies tell me what's going on, and why it smells like someone's gas tank is leaking?"

Flora had almost forgotten Officer Hendricks's promise that an officer would be patrolling her road a couple of times each night for the next week, but it seemed *he* hadn't forgotten, and she had never been so grateful to see the police as she was right then.

EPILOGUE

Flora stared at the crackling fire, feeling the heat on her skin. It made her face feel dry and stretched taut, but she couldn't bring herself to back away.

"It's a nice night for this," Grady said. She turned her head to look at him. He was sitting in a camp chair—she now had four of them. They somehow seemed to keep multiplying—drinking a beer while he watched the flames. She stepped back far enough to sink into the chair next to him. Across the fire from them, Violet was throwing a few more pieces of wood in, while Sydney hacked at a big tree limb with a hatchet. After Harriet's arrest, Violet had invited Sydney out to brunch with them, and the two of them exchanged stories about Nick and

Harriet, both the good and the bad. Flora had felt like the odd one out until Violet threw an arm around her shoulders and said, "You know what this means right? After what we went through together, we've all got to be best friends now. This is the sort of crazy shared experience that bonds people for life."

She got the feeling Sydney didn't have many friends, because he had seemed very touched by the pronouncement. She wondered what the past two years had been like for him, between losing his best friend, someone he had grown up with, and suspecting he knew who had killed him but being unable to prove it or even have the closure of a body. At least it was all over, now.

"Looks like you've got a visitor," Grady said, nodding toward the driveway. The bonfire was in the back portion of the yard, which she had finally cleaned up after Officer Hendricks came out to remove the crime scene tape. Now, a lone figure was shuffling across the yard towards them, coming from the road. She got up to meet him partway.

"Hi, Tim," she said. "How are you doing tonight?"

"You kids aren't supposed to be here," he warned, looking at her without recognition. "Old Mr. Barton won't be happy."

He didn't come by every night, but it happened often enough that it had become routine. She and Beth speculated it was because the house was inhabited for the first time in years, and a part of him still thought it should be empty. The dissonance brought him back to the years when he had helped his neighbors chase intruders away. She was glad she had gotten the security cameras—they alerted her to his presence, so she could go outside and make sure he didn't get hurt. Beth usually knew when her husband left the house, but even she wasn't perfect.

"Mr. Barton doesn't live here anymore," she told him gently. "I'm Flora, remember? I'm your new neighbor. I think Beth is probably worried about you, so why don't we head back to your house?"

She took his elbow and guided him back across the grass toward the road. He moved slowly, and she took the chance to glance back at the bonfire and her friends. Real friends, she thought. Violet had already had her back when it counted twice, and Grady had helped her escape from a madman with a gun back when he barely knew her. Violet was right—that sort of experience did form bonds. Despite everything that had happened, she was happy here, with her friends and her house, and her whole future spread out in front of her. With a little luck, things would be straightforward from here on out and this property didn't have any other surprises in store for her.

Printed in Great Britain
by Amazon

28179929R00067